Zoe's Rescue Zoo

With special thanks to Natalie Doherty

Text Copyright © 2016 by Hothouse Fiction
Illustrations Copyright © 2016 by Sophy Williams

ISBN 978-1-338-19447-0
10 9 8 7 6 5 4   17 18 19 20 21

Printed in the U.S.A.   40
This edition first printing 2017

Zoe's Rescue Zoo
The Sleepy Snowy Owl

Amelia Cobb

Illustrated by **Sophy Williams**

Scholastic Inc.

Chapter One
A Snowy Surprise

Zoe Parker wrapped her woolly scarf snugly around her neck and brushed a flurry of snowflakes from the front of her coat.

"Brrr! It feels so wintry today!" she said, shivering.

"Well, it *is* the start of December,"

replied her mom, Lucy, smiling and rubbing her hands together to stay warm.

"It's my favorite time of year," added Zoe's Great-Uncle Horace. "And today is the perfect day for a walk with my two favorite people! The Rescue Zoo always looks rather magical with a dusting of snow and a few Christmas lights. Don't you think, Zoe?"

Zoe grinned at him. "Definitely!" she said, reaching out to hold hands with him through her mittens. "I love this time of year too. I'm so glad you're back for Christmas and New Year's, Great-Uncle Horace."

"So am I, Zoe!" Great-Uncle Horace replied, beaming. "I do love going on adventures around the world, but there's no place quite like home. Especially at

Christmastime!"

Just as he said this, there was a very
noisy trumpeting sound behind them. Zoe
spun round to see Bertie, the silly young
elephant, inside his enclosure.

Great-Uncle Horace chuckled. "And
it sounds like Bertie is pleased too," he
added, winking at Zoe.

Zoe giggled at the funny little elephant.
Going out for an early Sunday morning
stroll was always lots of fun when you
had a very special home like Zoe did.
She and her family weren't just visiting
the Rescue Zoo—they actually lived
there!

Great-Uncle Horace was a famous
explorer and animal expert. He had met
so many lost, injured, and endangered
animals on his travels that he had decided
to set up the Rescue Zoo. Now it was a
safe home for hundreds of animals that
had needed help, just like Bertie.

Zoe's mom, Lucy, was Great-Uncle
Horace's niece and the Rescue Zoo
vet. Because she needed to be close to
the animals at all times in case of an
emergency, she and Zoe lived in a little

cottage just at the edge of the zoo.
This meant that Zoe was only ever a
few minutes away from all her favorite
animals. Zoe's bedroom window even
looked out on the enclosures, so she
woke up every morning to the sound
of the animals squawking, roaring, and
grunting!

Just like her mom and great-uncle,
Zoe loved animals, so she completely
adored her amazing home. This morning
it looked even more beautiful than usual.
It was a chilly day but the sky was very
bright and blue. There was a light dusting
of white snow on the branches of the
trees and the redbrick path. Some of the
zookeepers had hung garlands of holly,
ivy, and mistletoe along the fences so
that the zoo would look especially festive

when the gates opened to the visitors later that morning.

As they walked on, there was a tiny squeak from inside Zoe's coat. A gray, furry little head with fuzzy ears and big eyes popped out above her collar. "Is it time for lunch yet, Zoe? We've been walking for ages and ages!"

Zoe nuzzled the soft, fluffy head with her cheek. "No we haven't, Meep! And we've only just eaten breakfast!" she whispered with a smile, being careful not to let her mom and Great-Uncle Horace overhear. "And *you* haven't been doing any walking. You've been cuddled up inside my coat since we left home!"

"That's because I want to stay nice and warm!" squeaked Meep. "I don't like walking on the snow. It makes my paws cold."

On her sixth birthday, Zoe had discovered something magical. She had found out that animals can understand people and can talk to them. Most people don't understand animals, but Zoe had found out that she *could*! It was Zoe's most special secret. She'd never told another person—not even her mom!

Her amazing gift had made growing up in a zoo even more fun. Whenever no one else was around, Zoe loved chatting with the animals, from the tiniest tree frog to the biggest hippopotamus. And of all the animals at the Rescue Zoo, Meep was her favorite. He was a tiny gray mouse lemur, with huge golden eyes, an adorable little nose, and a long, curling tail. Unlike all the other animals at the zoo, Meep lived in the cottage with Zoe and her mom. He and Zoe went everywhere together.

Zoe dug deep in her coat pocket and pulled out a handful of seeds. "I thought you might get hungry," she whispered to Meep, "so I brought along a snack for you, just in case." She giggled as Meep stuffed the nuts and seeds straight into his mouth, making his cheeks puff up like a hamster.

"Zoe, why don't we head out of the zoo today?" suggested Great-Uncle Horace. "There's always lots of wonderful wildlife in the woods."

"OK!" replied Zoe with a smile. She followed the path around to the right, past the koalas and the flying foxes, toward a side gate that led out of the zoo and into some woodland. Great-Uncle Horace looked after the woods too, but they weren't part of the zoo grounds. And, unlike the zoo, they were left to grow wild. Zoe found the woodland mysterious and exciting!

She stepped carefully through the snowy bushes, keeping an eye out for any movement. Zoe knew that the field mice and hedgehogs would be hibernating at this time of year, but there would still be wild rabbits and hares running around, as well as pheasants.

Great-Uncle Horace glanced up and whistled to a large vivid-blue bird with huge feathery wings, flying along above them. At his whistle, she swooped down through the trees and perched on his shoulder. This was Kiki, Great-Uncle Horace's hyacinth macaw. She went with him on all his travels.

"Oh, look!" Great-Uncle Horace said cheerily as they walked farther into the woods. "See that flash of red up ahead?

A robin! One of my favorite birds. Apart from Kiki, of course!" He grinned and gently patted the bird's head as she bobbed on his shoulder.

"Oh yes, I see him!" said Lucy.

Zoe peered through the trees and saw the robin pecking at some juicy-looking berries on a bush. "Is that what robins eat in winter?" she asked.

"Oh, robins are very clever creatures. They never have any trouble finding enough to eat, even at the coldest time of the year," replied Great-Uncle Horace. "They'll nibble on winter fruit and seeds, and if the ground isn't frozen, they'll dig around for worms."

"Those berries look tasty!" Meep squeaked into Zoe's ear.

Before Zoe could stop him, she felt

Meep leap off her
and watched
him scamper
toward the
bush. Startled,
the robin
quickly
fluttered
away as Meep
greedily helped
himself to the
berries.

"Meep!" called
Zoe, running ahead
of her mom and Great-Uncle Horace to
chase after the playful little lemur. "Come
back here!" But as she got to the bush,
something caught her eye on the ground
beside it. She frowned and crouched down

to get a better look. "What's this?" she murmured to herself.

Meep stopped gobbling berries and peered down at the ground. There was a shallow hole dug into the earth, with a few white feathers scattered inside it. Just visible in the center of the hole was something small, pale, and round.

"Zoe? What did you find?" called
Lucy.

Zoe stared at the object. "I think . . . I
think I've found a nest—with an *egg*
inside it!" she replied.

Quickly, Great-Uncle Horace and Lucy
made their way over. Zoe knew it could
be very serious for an egg to be left alone
before it had hatched—especially in cold
weather. Luckily, the bush had sheltered it
so that there was no snow inside the nest.

"Goodness, you're right, Zoe!" said
Great-Uncle Horace.

Very gently, he bent over and picked up
the egg. He held it carefully in both palms
so that they could all look at it closely.
It was smooth and creamy white, with
no speckles or marks on the shell. On
his shoulder, Kiki let out a loud squawk.

Zoe knew it meant she was concerned
about the egg being left alone.

"Where do you think it came from,
Great-Uncle Horace?" Zoe asked. "Is it
a robin egg?"

"If I'm not mistaken, this is a snowy
owl egg!" Great-Uncle Horace told her.

"How on earth did it end up here? We don't have any snowy owls living in these woods, or at the Rescue Zoo . . ."

"It's very rare to find a wild snowy owl this far south," Lucy agreed. "I would guess that the mother got lost and decided to lay her egg here before trying to find her way back home."

Great Uncle-Horace nodded. "This egg has been abandoned, I'm afraid."

They both looked very serious.

"But . . . but that means this is a *lucky* egg, doesn't it?" Zoe said. "Of all the places in the whole world it could have been laid, it was laid here! In the woods next to the Rescue Zoo!"

Both Great-Uncle Horace and Lucy started laughing. "You're absolutely right, Zoe," said Lucy, giving her a hug. "It is a *very* lucky egg indeed! And it's unusual for us to find a new arrival so close to home."

"That's true! I usually have to travel to the other side of the world to find them," chuckled Great-Uncle Horace.

"So does that mean we can keep it?" asked Zoe hopefully. She'd met lots of different owls at the zoo, but never a snowy owl.

"Of course! We'll take it straight to the aviary, where all the Rescue Zoo birds live. It needs to be kept in an incubator until it hatches. It's very important to keep this little egg nice and warm," explained Great-Uncle Horace. "In fact, Zoe, maybe we could wrap it up in your scarf to take it back to the zoo?"

"Of course!" said Zoe immediately. She pulled off her woolly scarf and Great-

Uncle Horace wound it gently around the egg. Then he placed it carefully in Zoe's arms.

They headed out of the woods and back toward the zoo. Zoe led the way to the aviary, holding the egg proudly. All the zoo animals they passed were eager to know what they were up to!

"We've found a snowy owl egg!" Zoe whispered, whenever she could be sure that her mom and Great-Uncle Horace weren't in earshot. "We're going to look after it until it hatches, and then we'll all have a new friend!"

The aviary was a huge enclosure, full of different trees, plants, and colorful flowers. A winding stream ran through it for the birds to drink from. Zoe could hear the aviary before she could see it, because hundreds of birds were cheeping, tweeting, and squawking to one another! It was breakfast time and Alison, the bird-keeper, was scattering handfuls of seeds on the ground. Several birds were perched on her head and shoulders.

Alison waved when she saw Zoe approaching. "Good morning! What brings you here so early, Zoe?" she called.

"Hi, Alison! We've brought you a present," Zoe replied, grinning.

Alison was amazed to see the snowy owl egg wrapped inside Zoe's scarf! Quickly, Great-Uncle Horace explained how Zoe had discovered the nest on their morning walk.

Alison gently took the egg and held it up to a special light so she could find out the size of the little chick inside. "I'll get

the incubator ready right away," Alison
said. "I'd say this egg will be ready to
hatch in a week or so, as long as we keep
it nice and warm until then."

As Alison, Lucy, and Great-Uncle
Horace discussed all the different things
they'd need for the arrival of the baby
owl, Zoe and Meep slipped a little farther
into the aviary. Zoe wanted to say a
quiet hello to her bird friends, including
Cyril, an emerald-green lovebird, and
Ruby, a friendly macaw with beautiful
red feathers. She knew that Meep would
be eager to "help" the birds finish their
breakfast seeds—and he wasn't the only
one! Kiki had hopped straight down from
Great-Uncle Horace's shoulder and was
helping herself to the seeds scattered on
the ground. Zoe giggled as a tiny, brave

fairy-wren with a splash of purple on her neck chattered angrily at Kiki, who was at least ten times her size.

"I'm so excited that we're going to have a snowy owl at the zoo at last! I've always wanted to take care of one. They're really beautiful birds," Alison was saying happily. "I can't wait!"

"Me too!" said Zoe. "Alison, do you think I could help you watch over the egg until it hatches? I've never taken care of an egg before."

"Of course, Zoe," Alison replied. "As long as your mom doesn't mind?"

"Not at all!" answered Lucy, smiling. "If it wasn't for you, Zoe, we'd never have found the egg in the first place. So I think it only seems fair that you get to help take care of it."

"Just think, Zoe—with a little bit of luck, you might even be there when the egg hatches!" added Alison.

Zoe smiled. She really, really hoped so!

Chapter Two
Ollie Arrives!

For the next three days, Zoe visited the
aviary before she went to school and
rushed straight back there as soon as she
got home. It had snowed again that week
and was very cold outside, but the little
room where the incubator was set up
was always warm and snug. Zoe looked

forward to going to the aviary all day long—especially because Alison made her a nice big mug of hot chocolate as soon as she got there!

The incubator was a small, clear plastic box lit by several warm bulbs. The egg sat in the middle of the box, and Alison showed Zoe how to check the thermometer on its side, to make sure it was at the right temperature. She also explained that Zoe needed to turn the egg very carefully once a day and keep a close eye out for any movement. Zoe got a thrill of excitement in her tummy on the third day when she saw the egg wobble very slightly. "It moved!" she cried.

"Not long now before our little snowy owl is here, Zoe!" replied Alison, smiling.

On Wednesday night, Zoe had just

snuggled up in bed, with Meep curled
up by her feet, when the phone rang
downstairs in the kitchen. Zoe heard the
murmur of her mom's voice, and then she
called up the stairs. "Zoe! It's for you!"

Zoe jumped out of bed and quickly ran
downstairs.

"It's Alison!" said her mom, grinning
as she held out the
phone.

"Hello?" said Zoe
eagerly.

"Zoe! I'm sorry to
call so late. I hope
you weren't already
asleep!" Alison
said breathlessly.
"The egg has
started to hatch!

27

If you're quick, you'll make it just in time."

"Mom! The egg's hatching!" Zoe cried. "Can we go?"

"Of course!" Lucy said. "Get dressed, and we'll run there together."

Zoe threw on the jeans and sweater she'd been wearing earlier, jammed a woolly hat on her head, and grabbed her coat and boots. Together, she and her mom raced down the path to the aviary, with Meep scampering along behind them. When they got there, Alison ushered them into the incubator room and they all gathered around it.

"Oh, wow! Look!" Zoe gasped, pointing at the egg.

It was wriggling from side to side, and as Zoe watched, a piece of shell broke off from the top of the egg. She held her breath as another, bigger fragment of shell cracked away. Soon a tiny, fluffy, dark gray head appeared, cheeping faintly.

"There you are!" whispered Zoe. On her shoulder, Meep squeaked in excitement.

Alison helped the little owlet break its way out of the shell, and gently scooped it up in a soft blanket. It looked like a ball of fuzz. Zoe smiled as the owl slowly, sleepily, blinked its eyes.

Lucy and Alison carefully checked the little owl. "He's a boy, and he's perfectly healthy!" said Lucy. "Would you like to hold him, Zoe?"

Zoe made a little cradle with her hands and Alison gently passed the owlet to her. Zoe carefully stroked the owl's soft, fluffy head. "He feels so light and fragile," she said. "But he's not white! Are you sure he's a snowy owl, Alison?"

"I'm sure!" Alison reassured her, smiling. "Snowy owl chicks are born with a layer of dark, fuzzy down, but he'll grow lovely white feathers soon enough. And he'll get stronger and heavier as he grows older. Fully grown snowy owls can be very powerful. They need to be tough to survive winters in the arctic and hunt for their food!"

As Alison and Lucy chatted about the little owl's diet, Zoe whispered to him quietly. "I'm Zoe!" she told him. "And this is my friend Meep. We're both really excited to meet you!"

"What's your name?" asked Meep.

The tiny owl shook his fluffy head with a puzzled chirp.

"He doesn't have a name yet, Meep. He's only just hatched!" Zoe explained, smiling. "That means you can pick one yourself! Maybe we can help you choose? How about ... Orlando?" The owl cocked his little head to one side, thinking. "You don't seem sure about that one," said Zoe. "OK, maybe ..."

"Otis?" suggested Meep. "Or ... Oswald?"

"What about Ollie?" Zoe added.

The little owl paused, then cheeped brightly. "Ollie it is!" said Zoe, giggling quietly. "I think we're going to have lots of fun together, Ollie."

"Well, he seems very happy already!" commented Lucy, looking over and smiling at them. "Have you thought of any names yet, Zoe?"

"Um . . . can we call him Ollie?" Zoe asked.

"That's nice! Ollie the snowy owl," said Alison, trying the name out. "Perfect."

"Well, I think we'd better leave Ollie to get some rest," said Lucy. "And it's way past your bedtime too, Zoe! You can come back to visit after school tomorrow."

"And it's the Christmas holidays in a couple of weeks, isn't it?" added Alison.

Zoe nodded eagerly. "Yes! So I'll have lots of spare time to spend with Ollie. As long as that's OK with you, Alison?"

"Of course, Zoe. You were one of the very first people Ollie ever set eyes on," Alison replied. "Sometimes young birds can think that the first thing they see when they're born must be their mother! I can already tell you're going to have a really special bond with him."

As Zoe and her mom walked back through the zoo to the cottage, Lucy stopped to chat briefly to the keeper at the hippo enclosure, so Zoe had a chance to talk to Meep.

"Ollie is *so* cute, isn't he?" she whispered excitedly. "I can't wait to see him again."

Meep nodded. "This is going to be the best Christmas ever!" the little lemur squeaked.

"*And* the best New Year's!" Zoe added.

"Remember, Great-Uncle Horace is planning a special New Year's Eve celebration. It's going to be exactly ten years since the Rescue Zoo opened, so it's also our anniversary!"

As well as the arrival of the mysterious snowy owl egg, the New Year's Eve celebration was all anyone at the zoo could talk about—zookeepers *and* animals! Great-Uncle Horace had announced it just after he'd arrived home from his last adventure. Since then, Zoe and Meep had been eagerly waiting for him to tell them more.

"Oh yes!" squeaked Meep, clapping his paws together. "I'd forgotten about that, Zoe. I hope there'll be lots of tasty treats for me to eat. Bananas, blueberries, sunflower seeds . . ."

Zoe chuckled. "Well, maybe we can ask him now. Look, there he is!" she whispered, nodding at the path ahead. Great-Uncle Horace was strolling toward them, a long, thick knitted scarf wrapped several times around his neck. Kiki was perched on his shoulder. Zoe's mom caught up with them as he approached.

"Goodness me, you're both out very late, my dears! I would have thought you'd be tucked up in bed by now, Zoe. Is everything all right?" Great-Uncle Horace asked, looking worried.

"Everything's fine! We just came from the aviary. Zoe, do you want to tell Great-Uncle Horace the good news?" said Lucy.

Zoe explained that the snowy owl egg had finally hatched! She felt a flush of pride as she described how she'd held the tiny owlet for the first time. Great-Uncle Horace was delighted.

"Well done, Zoe! I'll go and pay the little guy a visit right away. And *I've* got some exciting news too!" he told them. "I've just made the final arrangements for our New Year's Eve celebrations. We're going to have a huge fireworks display! I've ordered three big boxes of rockets,

pinwheels, and fountains, all the way from China. They are all special low-noise fireworks, so they won't upset the animals but will still look splendid. The delivery should arrive in the next few days. And we'll have a fireworks expert to put the display on for us!"

"Fireworks!" cried Zoe, grinning at Great-Uncle Horace. "I love fireworks. And can we have sparklers too?"

"It wouldn't be a proper fireworks display without sparklers, my dear! I've ordered two hundred, which should be plenty for all the zoo's visitors," Great-Uncle Horace told her with a smile.

"Fireworks? Oh, dear. Where will we store them all, Mr. Higgins?" asked a voice from behind Zoe.

Zoe felt Meep bristle angrily in her

arms. It was Mr. Pinch, the grumpy zoo manager, who was doing his final check of the zoo for the night. "I'm concerned we might not have room for lots of big boxes, sir," Mr. Pinch continued. "The zoo is already very messy at the moment because of all the Christmas presents that have been bought for the animals."

"Not at all, my dear Mr. Pinch. Christmas is for everyone, including the animals!" Great-Uncle Horace told him happily. "And the fireworks are very important. We need to celebrate the zoo's anniversary properly! And there's plenty of room for the fireworks in the storage shed behind the aviary. I'll supervise the delivery myself. In fact, I'll go there now, before I visit our new snowy owl, and make sure it's ready for the delivery."

Zoe could see that Mr. Pinch still wasn't happy about the idea, but he nodded grudgingly. Zoe was *so* excited now. She couldn't wait for the school semester to finish and the Christmas holidays to begin. There was just so much to look forward to!

Chapter Three
Christmas Eve
Excitement

"One more sleep till Christmas!" Zoe
sang excitedly as she ran through the zoo,
enjoying the crunch of her footsteps in
the smooth, powdery snow.

Zoe's school had gone on break for
Christmas three days ago. Since then,

she had been enjoying spending all of her free time visiting her animal friends around the Rescue Zoo.

Zoe had fed the penguins and the flamingos, played in the snow with the polar bears, and had helped to give the zebras a special bath so that their stripy coats were glossy and clean for Christmas Day. Last night, she and Meep had taken part in the annual Carol Concert, where all the zookeepers and lots of visitors had gathered around the huge Christmas tree in front of the zoo café to sing Christmas songs.

Zoe was feeling especially merry this morning, and it wasn't just because it was Christmas Eve! She and Meep were on their way to see little Ollie. It was a special day for him too. The adorable baby owl had grown much bigger and stronger over the last few weeks, and his dark, fuzzy down was starting to be replaced by thick white feathers, just as Alison had said it would. In fact, Alison was so pleased with his progress that she'd decided Ollie was ready to live with the other Rescue Zoo birds. Today was the day he would be leaving the incubation room and moving into the aviary!

The little owl was waiting for Zoe when she arrived, and twittered excitedly when he saw her.

"I *know* you're moving today!" chuckled Zoe, stroking his soft little head. "Meep and I came as soon as we could. I just had to wrap my mom's Christmas present before we left."

Ollie chirped curiously.

"Oh, that's one of the nicest things about Christmas Day! Everyone gives one another presents," explained Zoe. It was funny to think that Ollie had never had a Christmas before! "I know—why don't I bring *you* a present tomorrow? Then you can see what it's all about," she said, and giggled as the little owl puffed his feathery chest up with pride.

"Hi, Zoe!" said Alison, popping her head inside the incubation room. "You're here nice and early. That's great—we can take Ollie into the main part of the aviary right away! It's funny—he's been chirping very cheerfully all morning. It's almost as if he understands that something exciting is happening today. I know that must sound silly!" Alison said, shaking her head and smiling. Zoe had to

hide her laughter, because, of course, Ollie
did know!

Alison handed Zoe a special red glove
made from thick, padded material. "I
wear these all the time. They keep your
hands from getting scratched by the birds'
sharp claws," she explained.

Zoe put the glove on and
held it out straight, in
front of where Ollie
was huddled.

With a bit of encouragement, the owlet hopped onto the glove and gripped the padded material. As Zoe carried him carefully through to the main part of the aviary, the little owl fluttered his wings and hooted excitedly. His eyes were wide as he stared around the beautiful enclosure.

"Isn't it nice?" Zoe whispered. "And look—all the other birds are excited to meet you too, Ollie!"

The rest of the aviary was just as eager and curious about the new arrival as he was about them! Zoe giggled as wrens, woodpeckers, and finches swooped around her head, chirping a friendly greeting to Ollie. Cyril and Ruby fluttered right up to them and twittered hello. Quietly, Zoe introduced Ollie to them.

"Goodness, he's making friends already!" Alison said with a laugh. "Why don't you set him down on this tree branch here, Zoe? That way he can get used to his new surroundings."

Zoe carefully lowered her glove so that Ollie could hop onto the branch. The little owl was chattering and hooting nonstop at all the colorful birds flying past him. Zoe grinned, feeling relieved. Ollie seemed to love his new home already!

Zoe wished she could stay at the aviary all day long, but when her tummy started rumbling, she knew it was time to head home for lunch. Meep was having fun at the aviary too, but he was always ready for his next meal! So, after waving good-bye to Alison and Ollie, Zoe scooped

Meep up and ran down the path toward the cottage.

There was a buzz of chatter in the living room as Zoe pushed open the front door and stepped inside. Around the table sat her mom, Great-Uncle Horace, and several of the zookeepers, nibbling cookies and sipping cups of tea.

"Zoe! There you are. There's some lunch for you in the kitchen," said Lucy. "And we've saved you a cookie for afterward!"

"What are you all doing?" Zoe asked, seeing several pads of paper and pens on the table.

"Oh, we're planning the New Year's Eve celebration!" explained Great-Uncle Horace. "Come and join us, Zoe. I know you're going to have lots of good ideas."

Zoe grabbed the plate of sandwiches from the fridge and a banana for Meep, and they joined the group around the table.

"We thought we'd start the evening with hot chocolate for everyone by the polar bear enclosure," Great-Uncle Horace told her. "That's where our fireworks expert will start the display, safely away from the animals. But first we thought we'd have a little show. We might let some of the animals show off their special tricks and talents! And I'll tell the story of how each one came to live at the zoo."

Zoe thought this sounded wonderful, and as the group continued to swap ideas, an idea of her own popped into her head. New Year's Eve was still a week away. Ollie might have started flying by then!

If he had, maybe he could take part in the show too.

Tomorrow, I'll ask him if he'd like that, she thought, taking a bite of her sandwich. *When I give him his Christmas present!*

Chapter Four
A Special Present

"I'm stuffed!" said Zoe, dropping her
fork onto her empty plate and pushing
it away. "That apple pie was so yummy,
Mom!"

"I very much agree!" added Great-
Uncle Horace, patting his stomach.
"Delicious."

It was Christmas Day, and Zoe's family had exchanged presents before sitting down at the kitchen table to eat a huge lunch. Zoe secretly thought that Great-Uncle Horace looked like Santa Claus today, with his white beard flowing over his bright red Christmas sweater!

"Are you sure you don't want second helpings?" suggested Lucy. "There's plenty left."

Great-Uncle Horace looked thoughtful. "Well, I might have room for just another tiny piece . . ."

Zoe shook her head. "I think I'd pop! Besides, I was wondering if I could go and say hello to Ollie. I want to see how he's settling in to the aviary. And I got him a Christmas present!"

"That's fine, Zoe, just don't be late getting back. That penguin movie you love is on TV tonight, so I thought we could all watch it together," Lucy told her.

"And we could open those fancy chocolates you gave me, Zoe!" added Great-Uncle Horace, winking at her. Great-Uncle Horace had a serious sweet tooth!

"Great! I won't be long," Zoe promised. She pulled on her coat and the new matching purple-and-blue-striped hat and scarf her mom had given her for Christmas, and picked up Ollie's present from by the front door. Meep followed alongside her as they headed outside. It was frosty underfoot, so Zoe walked carefully, doing her best not to skid or slip.

Zoe had a special necklace that let her

into any enclosure in the zoo. She used her necklace's special silver paw-print pendant to open the aviary gate, and she and Meep slipped inside. The air was filled with cheerful chirping and tweeting. The birds were celebrating Christmas too!

"Merry Christmas, Ollie!" she called as she spotted the little owlet. Ollie fluttered his wings happily when he saw her and hooted back.

"I did get some awesome presents, thank you!" replied Zoe, grinning. "This hat and scarf, which are keeping me toasty warm, and some books, and a big set of markers! And I didn't forget to bring *your* present, Ollie."

She placed the parcel in front of Ollie, giggling as his big eyes opened even wider in amazement. With Zoe's help, Ollie used his tiny beak and claws to rip off the wrapping paper. Inside was a bag of mealworms and two small pieces of wood, each shaped like the letter *T*.

"They're perches! They're to help you practice your flying," Zoe explained. "These long parts are pushed straight down into the ground, a yard or so apart. And you perch on the flat parts here. You can try flying from one perch to another—and the better you get, the farther apart we can set them up!"

Ollie loved his presents, especially the perches! He hooted eagerly at Zoe until she agreed to set them up for him right away. Zoe gently lifted him onto one of the perches, and smiled as Ollie fluttered his feathers as hard as he could, lifting himself into the air. He almost made it over to the other perch, but his little wings weren't quite strong enough, and

he started to lose height just before he got there. Zoe had to catch him and carry him the rest of the way.

"Don't worry, you'll be able to do this all by yourself in no time," she reassured him. "You're so close now. And if you're flying well enough on New Year's Eve, I was wondering if you'd like to take part in the show."

Ollie looked curious, so Zoe explained Great-Uncle Horace's idea to introduce animals to the visitors. "Usually, Great-Uncle Horace is the person who finds animals needing a home at the Rescue Zoo. He's going to talk about all the other animals in the show. And since it's so rare to find a snowy owl like you so far south, I bet everyone would be really interested to hear your story, about how

I found you in your egg right here in the woods by the zoo! I thought maybe I could even be the one to introduce you— if you'd like to do it, that is."

Ollie hooted sleepily, and Zoe noticed that his eyes were drooping a little as she spoke. *He must be tired from his first try at flying!* she thought, smiling to herself. *He's so cute.*

"I could tell all the visitors how you were hatched here at the zoo, and then you could do a little bit of flying. Everyone would love you!" she finished. "What do you think?"

Ollie perked up a bit, and chirped back excitedly. Zoe smiled. "I'm so glad you like the idea! And if you keep practicing, you'll definitely be ready in time for the show," she told him. "It will be so much

fun, Ollie. New Year's Eve is one of my
favorite nights of the whole year. Mom
always lets me and Meep stay up until
midnight! We're sometimes a bit sleepy
the next day, but we don't mind."

As she said this, the little owl's eyes
drooped again, and he yawned. Zoe
laughed. "It looks like you're sleepy *now*,
Ollie!" she said.
"Aren't you
getting enough
sleep? Is the
aviary too
noisy?"

Hooting
animatedly
now, Ollie
pointed his
wing to a group

of birds who were roosting at the back
of the aviary, their heads tucked under
their wings as they slept. "So you're
staying awake at nighttime to play with
the nocturnal birds, like the hawks, the
nightingales, and the barn owls," said
Zoe, beginning to understand. "But
you're not going to sleep in the daytime
either, because you're so excited about
making friends with all the other birds,
and spending time with me and Meep!
You don't want to miss anything, do you,
Ollie?"

The little owlet shook his head firmly,
chirping enthusiastically. Zoe reached
out to give his feathers a gentle stroke.
"Well, Meep and I love visiting you too!"
she told him, smiling. "But you've got to
be careful, Ollie. Snowy owls are special.

Most owls are nocturnal, but Great-Uncle Horace told me that snowy owls can choose whether to sleep in the daytime or at night. And you do need to make sure you get plenty of sleep! You don't want to tire yourself out. You might get sick, or fall asleep while you're flying and have an accident."

"Sleeping can be fun," added Meep helpfully. "I love it when Zoe tucks me in and tells me a bedtime story! My favorite is about a little lemur, like me, who lives in a magical banana tree. It grows as many bananas as you like, no matter how many you eat! I always have nice dreams about bananas after that story. Mmm . . ."

But Ollie didn't seem very interested in sleeping or in having nice dreams!

With a cheerful tweet, he fluttered his wings and tried once again to fly to the other perch.

"It looks like Ollie is determined to be ready for the New Year's Eve show, Meep!" Zoe whispered with a giggle. She couldn't wait for it either!

Chapter Five
A Sleepy Problem

Three days later, Zoe and Meep were on their way to visit Ollie again when they saw a delivery truck parked close to the aviary. Several delivery men were lifting three huge wooden crates from the back of the truck and stacking them up by the side of the path. There were colorful

Chinese symbols painted on the side of the crates.

"Meep, look! That must be the New Year's Eve fireworks," said Zoe. "Wow, it looks like there are hundreds of them!"

Great-Uncle Horace was there too, directing the boxes to where he wanted them. "Into the storage shed behind the aviary, please!" he said happily, signing a piece of paper that one of the delivery men handed him. "Not long to wait until we see these lighting up the whole sky! Our display is going to be splendid!"

"Mr. Pinch doesn't look very pleased, does he?" whispered Zoe, and Meep giggled playfully. The zoo manager was patching up a broken section of the aviary fence nearby, and watching the fireworks arrive with a very grumpy

expression on
his face.

"Ugh,
fireworks,"
Zoe heard
him mumble
to himself
crankily.
"Too bright.
They hurt
my eyes."

Great-
Uncle Horace
saw Zoe passing
and waved to her. "Good morning, my
dear!" he called. "Off to see our little
snowy owl? Alison tells me his flying has
really improved since Christmas Day—
thanks to your lovely present, no doubt!"

Zoe nodded. "He's getting much better!" she told him.

On her shoulder, Meep squeaked, "Ask him about the show, Zoe!"

Zoe took a deep breath. She hadn't spoken to Great-Uncle Horace yet about her idea to have Ollie taking part in the New Year's Eve celebrations.

"Actually," she began slowly, "I think he might even be good enough to take part in the show on New Year's Eve," she said. "And, well, I was wondering if I could introduce him. I could explain how I found the egg and helped look after it until it hatched. And then I could tell the visitors a little bit about him, and Ollie could do some flying at the end."

Great-Uncle Horace beamed. "Zoe, that is an excellent idea!" he replied.

He rummaged around in his pockets and found a notepad and pencil. "I will add you and Ollie to my list of performers right this minute, which makes it official!"

Zoe grinned. "Thanks, Great-Uncle Horace!" she said, running to give him a big hug. She couldn't wait!

As Great-Uncle Horace continued making the arrangements for New Year's Eve, Zoe and Meep went inside the aviary, excited to see Ollie. "We'll have to make sure Mr. Pinch doesn't hear us talking to the birds though, Meep. He's right outside the fence," Zoe whispered as they pushed open the gate.

As soon as Ollie saw them, he raised his feathery wings and fluttered into the air, almost as high as Zoe's head! The little owl was so excited about how much his

flying had improved, he let out a very
loud, high-pitched squeak. And all the
other birds seemed excited by the owlet's
progress too! Zoe giggled as Ruby and
Cyril ruffled their feathers and chirped
happily.

"Dear, oh, dear, why is there never any peace and quiet around here? That horrible squawking din is driving me crazy!" grumbled Mr. Pinch from the other side of the fence.

"Mr. Pinch is driving *me* crazy," chattered Meep rudely.

"Naughty Meep! It's a good thing he can't understand you," Zoe whispered.

Luckily, the noisy birdsong seemed to be too much for Mr. Pinch to bear. After another minute or two, he threw his tools down. "I'm going to send one of the zookeepers to finish this job. This racket is giving me a nasty headache," he snapped, stomping off.

"Good!" said Zoe as soon as he'd disappeared out of sight. "Grumpy old Mr. Pinch. Just ignore him, Ollie."

The little owl nodded but had suddenly fallen very quiet. "Is everything OK, Ollie?" Zoe asked anxiously, noticing the little owl settle back down onto his perch, his eyelids drooping. Suddenly, he opened his beak and let out a huge yawn!

"Oh, dear!" said Zoe. "You seem really tired, Ollie. Remember when we talked about you needing to get enough sleep?"

Next to Ollie, one of the tiny yellow canaries tweeted anxiously. "Ollie, Dot says you haven't slept all night!" said Zoe, listening carefully. "Is that true?"

Eagerly, if a bit sleepily, the little owl explained.

"Ollie, I know you get really excited about your flying," Zoe replied gently. "And you're doing really well! But if you're going to stay up the whole night with the nocturnal birds, you need to get some sleep in the daytime."

Just as she said this, the little bird's eyes closed. "Ollie?" said Zoe, realizing the little owl was asleep. "Ollie?"

He let out a little snore, and then, with a start, Ollie blinked awake again, looking around in confusion. Zoe couldn't help finding it really sweet, but she was a bit concerned.

"See, Ollie—you fell asleep!" she said. "You must be exhausted. If you're this tired, you might not feel up to taking part in the show . . ."

Ollie hooted quickly as soon as she spoke. "It's OK, don't worry! There are three days to go," Zoe told him. "As long as you get some rest before then, I know you'll be great in the show. But you need to decide *when* you're going to sleep! Do you want to be a night owl and sleep in the day? Or do you want to sleep at night?"

Ollie gave a puzzled chirp. Zoe listened as he explained, nodding. He told her that there were just too many fun things going on at the Rescue Zoo, at lots of different times. He didn't know how to choose!

"It's a shame that there are no other

snowy owls at the zoo who we could ask about when *they* like to sleep. But maybe some of the other birds in the aviary can help you decide. Meep and I can ask our other animal friends for advice too," suggested Zoe. She smiled as the little owl's eyes lit up. "Don't worry, Ollie. I promise we'll help you figure it out!"

Chapter Six
Animal Advice

Zoe and Meep started on their plan to help Ollie that very afternoon.

"Henry?" Zoe called, standing on her tiptoes by the fence outside the hippo enclosure. "Can we ask your advice about something?"

The little hippo waddled proudly up

to the fence, leaving muddy footprints behind him. Before Ollie, Henry had been the Rescue Zoo's newest arrival! Quickly, Zoe explained Ollie's problem to him. "When do *you* like to sleep?" Zoe asked.

Henry grunted cheerfully and Zoe nodded. "You love splashing around in

your mud bath all day, so you're sleepy by the time it starts to gets dark," she said thoughtfully. "And then you're up bright and early as soon as the sun comes up again, ready for lots more playing! Thanks, Henry."

Next, they visited the reptile house. Even though it was chilly outside, the iguanas and monitor lizards were curled up by the windows inside their warm, steamy enclosures, basking in the winter sunshine. They were eager to help Zoe. "You need the sun's light to keep your blood nice and warm. So that's why you like to be up in the daytime and sleep at night!" Zoe exclaimed, and the lizards nodded in agreement.

The third animal Zoe went to ask was drowsily having a sip of water. Zoe could tell that Arnold the aye-aye had been sleeping. He blinked his big yellow eyes at her as Zoe gently said, "Hi, Arnold! I'm just trying to help Ollie, our baby snowy owl, and I wanted to ask you something. He can't decide when the best time to go to sleep is. Why do you like sleeping in the daytime so much?"

Arnold yawned, showing off his long, pointy front teeth, rubbing his eyes as he answered. "Your sharp lemur eyes can see really well at night!" said Zoe, smiling. "And you're very shy, so you prefer to snooze while the other animals are awake. That's really helpful, Arnold. Now, go back to sleep!"

As Arnold settled back down to sleep
again, Zoe and Meep headed back
toward the aviary. As they neared the
fence, Zoe noticed a flash of deep blue
and a bright yellow beak. Kiki!

"It looks like Great-Uncle Horace is
in the aviary," she said quietly to Meep.
"We'll have to be careful not to let him
see us
talking to
Ollie, or any
of the other
birds."

Zoe used
her special
necklace to
open the
gate and
saw that

Great-Uncle Horace was tickling Ollie's fluffy feathers. "Hi, Great-Uncle Horace," she called.

"Hello, Zoe! I thought I'd come to pay this little fellow a visit. I can see you're doing an excellent job with his flying," he said, smiling. "And he seems extremely happy and settled. And he looks wonderful too. His white feathers are growing thicker every day!"

Zoe smiled. "I'm really enjoying helping him," she told Great-Uncle Horace.

Great-Uncle Horace nodded. "It's so nice to see our little rescued friend's progress, isn't it? Oh, I think Kiki and I will go and say hello to the hummingbirds before we go."

He waved good-bye and strolled through to the farthest area of the aviary, where

the hummingbirds had built their nests.
As soon as he was out of earshot, Zoe and
Meep crouched down beside Ollie. The
little owl hooted happily, but Zoe could
see that he was still looking tired.

"We've been asking lots of our animal
friends about when *they* sleep," she
explained. "But they all do different
things! Some like to be awake in the
sunshine. Some prefer the dark and the
quiet. There are lots of good things about
both!"

Ollie gave an enthusiastic but puzzled
hoot. He was still no closer to deciding
when *he* would choose as his regular time
to sleep! Zoe explained all the various
reasons the animals had given her for
when they slept, but Ollie just hooted
excitedly, hearing about all the amazing

different animals in the zoo, and asked when he might be able to meet them! Zoe could tell the little owl was no closer to settling on a sleep pattern.

"I'm a bit worried about Ollie," Zoe said to Meep quietly as they left the aviary. "I think I should make sure he doesn't overdo it and tire himself out, especially since he's so excited about being in the show! It might be my fault for making too much of it, and now he's not getting the rest he needs."

"Don't worry, Zoe," Meep squeaked reassuringly. "I'm sure he'll figure it out soon!"

But Zoe wasn't so sure. What would they do if the owlet couldn't sleep properly in the night *or* the day . . . ?

Chapter Seven
Ollie Saves the Day!

By the following evening, Zoe was more anxious than ever about poor Ollie. He'd fallen asleep in the middle of hooting a "hello" to Zoe that morning! But the little owlet was still so excited about the New Year's Eve show that he couldn't settle down to sleep properly.

Over dinner in the cottage, Zoe explained the problem to her mom—but she didn't mention that she could talk to Ollie, of course!

"I'm worried about Ollie. I don't think he's getting very much sleep," she said. "He seems to love living in the aviary with all the other birds, but he's having too much fun to rest!"

"The aviary is a very bright, colorful, noisy environment," agreed Lucy. "Perhaps he just needs to find a quiet, cozy corner and then he'll be able to relax. Maybe I could ask Alison to help him do that tonight?"

"Alison's busy tonight," Zoe said, remembering what the bird-keeper had told her earlier that day. "There are some other new baby birds that she needs to take care of—some parakeet eggs hatched this morning. But maybe *I* could go over to the aviary and help Ollie go to sleep?"

Lucy hesitated. "I'm not sure, Zoe. You've been spending so much time there recently that I think *you* might need an early night. Look—you're trying to hide a yawn, but I can see it! It's New Year's Eve in just a few days, and you're going to be up late then. If you're tired, you won't be able to enjoy yourself."

"Please, Mom?" begged Zoe. "If Ollie doesn't get some sleep soon, I'm worried he'll get sick. And he's so excited about being in the New Year's Eve show. It would be such a shame if people don't get to hear his story—he's so special. Please?"

Lucy finally nodded. "OK, Zoe. But just for an hour or two," she said. "And I'll be checking in with Alison to make sure everything's OK. I want you to be home by nine o'clock and then straight to bed for a good night's sleep yourself!"

"Thanks, Mom!" said Zoe gratefully.

After Zoe had washed the dishes, she pulled on her coat and grabbed her schoolbag, which she packed with some important things.

"What are those for?" squeaked Meep curiously.

"You'll see!" Zoe told him with a mysterious smile.

When Zoe and Meep arrived at the aviary a few minutes later, the nocturnal birds were fluttering awake, while the rest of the birds were settling down to sleep for the night. Ollie was flitting between them, not able to decide what to do. One moment he'd join a cluster of doves that was snuggling up quietly together, and they'd all coo at him welcomingly; the next, he'd catch sight of some corncrakes starting a game of chase around the aviary and want to join in!

"Ollie, we've come to help you get a good night's sleep," Zoe explained, reaching out and giving his feathers a gentle stroke. "I've brought a few things that might help."

She opened her schoolbag and pulled out a teddy bear, a warm blanket, and a book. "When I'm struggling to sleep, I give Meep a cuddle," she told Ollie. "So I thought you might like my old teddy bear, Walter, to snuggle up against. He's really soft and squishy!"

Zoe carried Ollie and all her things to

the very back of the aviary, where she
thought it might be quieter. She found
a cozy, dark corner, put the blanket on
the ground, and made it into a snug nest,
explaining that snowy owls in the wild
often make their nests on the ground, like
the one he was found in. She carefully
lifted Ollie into the middle of it. She
placed Walter next to the little owl and
then opened the book. "Mom usually
reads me a
bedtime story,"
she explained.
"Sometimes
Great-Uncle
Horace reads
them, but he
always does
funny voices

to make me laugh! Would you like me to try reading you a story?"

"She's really good at them!" added Meep.

Ollie cheeped eagerly, snuggling down in his blanket nest. Zoe sat down next to him, with Meep curled up on her lap, and started reading. "Once upon a time, there was a wizard . . ."

After the first chapter, Zoe heard a tiny snore—but it wasn't Ollie. It was Meep! The little lemur had fallen asleep. And Zoe realized she was also feeling very sleepy. She yawned, rubbing her eyes. It *was* nice and warm in the aviary, and it was so peaceful in this little corner. The gentle chirping of the birds had made her feel very relaxed. *Maybe I'll just close my eyes for ten minutes*, she thought . . .

Suddenly, there was a loud, urgent
hooting sound. Zoe's eyes sprang open
and she looked around. Ollie was flying
by her head, flapping his wings and
making as much noise as he possibly
could!

"Ollie, what's going on?" Zoe asked.

Ollie chirped and twittered noisily,

fluttering his wings to point beyond the fence. Zoe frowned as she realized how anxious the little owl was. "Ollie, what have you heard?" she asked. "Can you slow down? I don't understand what you're trying to tell me!"

But Ollie was too agitated to explain himself clearly! He kept screeching as loudly as he could. Zoe got to her feet and peered through the fence, trying to make out what Ollie was showing her. It was too dark for her eyes to see anything clearly, but suddenly she remembered what was behind the aviary.

"The fireworks are being kept in the storage shed back there," she said. "It must be something to do with that! I'd better go and have a look."

"I'm coming too!" Meep chattered.

They went out through the gate and walked around the back of the aviary toward the storage hut, squinting to see in the darkness. Zoe realized that she could see a light flickering and flashing ahead of her. *A flashlight*, she thought. But who was holding it? And what were they doing? *Maybe it's Great-Uncle Horace checking on the fireworks*, she thought. *But why would Ollie be so worried about that?*

The beam of flashlight suddenly lit up the storage shed door, and Zoe saw that it was swinging open, the padlock that Great-Uncle Horace had fixed on it lying broken on the ground. Zoe froze and listened carefully. She heard a muffled voice whisper, "Quick! Grab that box of rockets so we can get out of here before someone catches us!"

Zoe gasped, then clapped her hands over her mouth. She realized that someone had broken into the storage shed and was trying to steal the fireworks! Just then, she saw a flash of white in the semidarkness and felt a fluttering of wings beside her.

"Ollie!" she cried. The little owl had slipped out behind them when they'd left the aviary! "What are you doing?"

Ollie started hooting again as loudly as he could, and his noisy warning alerted all the other birds inside the aviary too!

Zoe saw that the canaries, the parrots, and the nightingales had all fluttered to the back of the aviary to see the intruders for themselves. Now they were joining in, tweeting and screeching as noisily and urgently as they could, and fluttering their wings toward the scene of the crime. The whole aviary was raising the alarm together!

It was so loud that Meep had his little paws pressed over his ears. "Zoe, what's going on?" the little lemur squeaked, rushing up onto her shoulder.

"Meep, we've got to run home and get Mom!" Zoe whispered desperately. "Some robbers are trying to steal the fireworks!"

Suddenly, she noticed more movement—the robbers were coming out of the storage shed! She fell back into the shadows, not sure what to do. What if they were dangerous? But little Ollie flapped toward them, screeching loudly!

"What's that?" Zoe heard an alarmed voice say.

"I–I think it's a ghost!" replied another voice, shaky with worry.

Just at that moment, Zoe heard footsteps coming down the path, and a very grumpy voice. "Those noisy, nuisance birds!" Mr. Pinch snapped. "What on earth is going on? I could hear that racket from the other side of the zoo!"

Zoe saw Mr. Pinch's face glaring at the birds over the fence. She'd never been so glad to see him! He spotted Ollie flapping and hooting near the storage hut.

"What on earth? How did that snowy owl get out of the aviary?"

But as he saw the other birds clustered at the back of the enclosure, squawking and fluttering too, Mr. Pinch's expression changed to one of puzzlement. He walked around the aviary to see what the birds were all getting so worked up about, and Zoe held her breath as he shone his flashlight toward the storage shed . . .

Quickly, Mr. Pinch grabbed his walkie-talkie. "Come in, all Rescue Zoo staff!" he shouted into the mouthpiece. "Robbery at the zoo! Everyone, come quickly!"

Just a few seconds later, the first zookeepers rushed down the path. Zoe, Meep, and Ollie watched in anxious anticipation as the thieves were stopped as they tried to sneak out through the zoo gates. Soon, three very red-faced teenage boys were being brought back to the aviary by some of the zoo staff.

"What are you trying to do with our fireworks?" Mr. Pinch demanded.

"We heard you had the best fireworks here. We just wanted to set a few off ourselves," mumbled one of the boys sheepishly.

"Well, it's a good thing we caught you!" announced Mr. Pinch. "These special fireworks are for the Rescue Zoo's New Year's Eve celebrations—a very important event. Thanks to my quick thinking, the show will go on!"

Zoe couldn't believe it. Mr. Pinch seemed to have changed his mind about the fireworks, now that he had stopped them from being taken! As she watched, Great-Uncle Horace arrived on the scene and congratulated Mr. Pinch on his good work in raising the alarm.

"We all know who *really* saved the day," Zoe whispered to Ollie, giving the little owlet a cuddle. "Your brilliant owl hearing meant those boys were caught! New Year's Eve would have been ruined if you hadn't raised the alarm!"

As she spoke, Ollie's little eyes closed. Zoe giggled. "You look ready for bed at last, after all that excitement," she said, and was relieved to see Ollie nod. He gently hooted that he might be ready to go to sleep now!

Chapter Eight
New Year's Eve

"Happy New Year!" called Zoe, waving at David, the elephant-keeper, as he walked past her with a tray of hot chocolate. Meep, perched on her shoulder, sniffed the air hungrily at the scent of the sweet drink.

"Almost, Zoe!" David called back,

smiling. "We've got another few hours to go first!"

It was finally New Year's Eve, and the Rescue Zoo was bustling with noise and people. Almost two hundred visitors had bought tickets to see the show, including lots of children from Zoe's class at school! Zoe grinned and waved as her friends Nicola and Jack walked past with their parents. Jack's face was painted like a crocodile with streaks of green and black, while Nicola's was covered in sparkly blue swirls like the wings of a butterfly.

Zoe thought the zoo looked amazing! Colorful banners had been hung up around the fences, with TEN YEARS OLD! painted on them, to let everyone know that today was the Rescue Zoo's tenth anniversary. As well as the face-painting, someone was making balloon animals, and along the path were stalls piled high with delicious things to eat. Zoe had already enjoyed a baked potato topped with melted cheese, and then a gooey chocolate brownie. She'd even let Meep nibble a few crumbs of the potato, which he was very pleased about!

Now Zoe was on her way to meet Alison. The animal show was about to start, and she was sure that Ollie was going to be a star! The little owl had told Zoe he'd decided to take lots of little naps throughout the day *and* night. That way, he'd always be well rested and alert in case the zoo needed him again! So he was back to his bright, eager self. Zoe found Alison behind the zoo café, where all the keepers and animals who were taking part in the show had gathered. Ollie was perched on Alison's red padded glove. Meep climbed down from Zoe's shoulder and waited with the other animals. Meanwhile, Zoe carefully put on another glove and took Ollie on her own hand as he hooted excitedly.

"It's time for the first part of our New Year's Eve celebrations!" announced Great-Uncle Horace, clapping his hands. "Everyone, gather around me, please."

Zoe watched as Great-Uncle Horace started the show by introducing Daisy, one of the giraffes. Daisy showed off her long

neck and stood
proudly while
Great-Uncle
Horace pointed out
her beautiful pattern
of patches and the
knobbly ossicones on
top of her head.

After that, three baby pygmy marmosets were brought out. The whole crowd gasped at the gorgeous babies, who were so small that they could perch together in her great-uncle's hands!

Great-Uncle Horace explained that pygmy marmosets are the world's smallest monkey, and talked about how he'd rescued their mother when the part of the rain forest she'd lived in had been cut down by people wanting the trees for firewood.

Zoe felt quite nervous when it was her turn to step forward and introduce Ollie. She saw her mom in the crowd, beaming at her encouragingly, and Alison gave her a big smile and a thumbs-up.

"And now, ladies and gentlemen, I'm very pleased to welcome my great-niece,

Zoe, who lives here at the zoo and knows it better than anyone—even me!" said Great-Uncle Horace. "Zoe's going to introduce one of our very newest arrivals at the Rescue Zoo."

Zoe held up her gloved hand and Ollie fluttered his wings happily. There was a gasp from the crowd.

"He's sooooo cute," said a boy in the front row.

"This is Ollie," said Zoe, but she could hear the nervous tremble in her voice. "Um, he's a snowy owl, and he's around four weeks old." Zoe spotted her mom again, and she was nodding and smiling at her encouragingly. Beside her, she heard Great-Uncle Horace whisper, "You're doing marvellously, Zoe! Why don't you explain how Ollie arrived at the zoo?"

Zoe took a deep breath. "A few weeks ago, I was out on a walk with my mom and Great-Uncle Horace," she explained to the crowd, and her voice was steadier this time. "I found a nest with an egg inside it, and it turned out to be a snowy owl nest. Snowy owls are really rare this far south. Everyone was worried because the egg had been abandoned, but we brought it back to the zoo, and I looked after it with Alison, the bird-keeper. We kept it warm in a special incubator, and Ollie hatched a few days later! Ollie's a

very special owl, because he's active in
the daytime *and* at night.

He loves eating
mealworms, but his
favorite thing to do
is practice flying."

Zoe held out her
arm, and right on cue,
Ollie fluttered his little wings
as hard as he could
and rose up from
Zoe's glove. The
crowd gasped
as the tiny owl
managed three
circles in the air
above her head,
before coming to
rest back on the glove.

"Well done, Ollie!" said Zoe, beaming.

"And well done, Zoe!" added Great-Uncle Horace, clapping enthusiastically. "Another round of applause for our wonderful animals! And now it's time for the next part of our evening—our special fireworks display, which will take place just over there, away from some of our more sensitive animal friends!"

Ollie hooted excitedly at Zoe. "I know—your first-ever fireworks display! I think you're going to like it!" replied Zoe in a whisper, grinning at the little owl.

Alison and Lucy came forward to congratulate Zoe on her part of the show, and Meep scampered over too.

"You were great, sweetheart!" said Lucy. "I'm so proud of you. And in front of that great big crowd too!"

Zoe grinned. "I was a bit nervous at first, but Ollie was amazing, wasn't he?" she said. "I knew everyone would be really interested in finding out more about him!"

"You were both great," Alison said. "You and Ollie make a fantastic team! Why don't you let me hold him now, so that you can go and get a sparkler? Looks like they're being handed out over there!"

"Oh, yes, please!" said Zoe excitedly. She passed Ollie to Alison, giving him one final wink, and then ran over to choose a sparkler, with Meep scampering at her heels. At the edge of the clearing, a lady was setting up the final fireworks. "That must be the fireworks expert Great-Uncle Horace hired!" Zoe whispered to Meep as he climbed up onto

her shoulder. "I bet that's a really fun job!"

After the crowd had had a chance to play with the sparklers, Great-Uncle Horace led the crowd in counting down the final minute to midnight and the brand-new year.

Zoe stood with her mom and Alison, with Meep in her arms and Ollie perched on Alison's glove. Meep and Ollie seemed even more excited than the people in the crowd! They both squealed happily as the countdown reached zero, and everyone yelled "Happy New Year!" together.

Right then, the first firework took off. Zoe gazed up as it soared high into the air and exploded into a shower of pink and orange sparks, followed by green and yellow, and then blue and purple.

Soon the whole sky was full of bright colors—and, incredibly, a few animal shapes too!

"Wow, look!" gasped Zoe, pointing. "Those yellow ones are in the shape of a lion with a big furry mane!"

"And those look like big blue dolphins!" added Lucy, nodding at the sky. "Isn't that amazing? I think these might be the best fireworks I've ever seen. We're so lucky that they didn't end up getting stolen!"

Zoe giggled as Ollie hopped up and down happily.

"We're so lucky that you were awake and that your sharp hearing meant you could raise the alarm, Ollie," she whispered. "And we're really, really lucky to live here at the Rescue Zoo! I can't wait to find out what new animals this year will bring!"

Read about Zoe's first animal adventure!

The cub blinked nervously at the crowd. He opened his mouth to reveal a row of white baby teeth and gave a squeaky growl. His little paws trembled and he looked very weak and frightened.

"Stand back, please!" Mr. Pinch announced as the visitors pushed forward to get a better look. "Make way for the vet."

Zoe's mom knelt down slowly next to the cub. "There, there, little one. I'm not going to hurt you," she soothed as she examined the lion's eyes, ears, teeth, tummy, and paws. The cub shrank away, snarling as fiercely as he could. Zoe's mom looked up. "You found him just in time, Uncle Horace. It looks like he hasn't eaten in weeks."

Zoe and Meep shared a worried look. The cub seemed confused and very scared. He kept turning his head from side to side, as if he was looking for someone in the crowd. Zoe desperately wanted to explain that everyone at the Rescue Zoo was really kind and wanted to help him. But she couldn't talk to him in front of the crowd—she had to keep the animals' secret.

Zoe felt a gentle tug on her hair, and realized it was Kiki trying to get her attention.

Great-Uncle Horace was standing next to her. Leaning closer, he whispered, "My dear, this little chap needs help. Will you promise to look after him for me?"

Zoe stared at her great-uncle and then nodded. "I promise. I'll try my very best to help the cub."

NEW AT THE ZOO

Zoe Parker has an amazing secret—she can talk to animals!

Her special talent comes in handy at her great-uncle's Rescue Zoo. Here, injured or endangered animals find a safe place to live.

These are no ordinary princesses...

The Secret Promise

The Wishing Pearl

The Moonlight Mystery

The Stolen Crystals

The Snow Jewel

The Magic Rings

The Lost Gold

The Shimmering Stone

...they're Rescue Princesses!

By Paula Harrison

SCHOLASTIC
scholastic.com

Available in print
and eBook editions

RESC

THE PUPPY PLACE

Read them all!

WHERE EVERY PUPPY FINDS A HOME

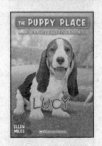